To Maddie

Best of Friends

Linda Rae School

:)

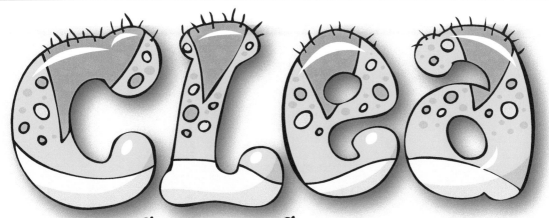

CLEO

THE CLEVER CATERPILLAR

written by Linda Rae Schaal ... illustrated by Don Sidle

Clea the Clever Caterpillar
Written by Linda Rae Schaal
Illustrated by Don Sidle
© 2021 Linda Rae Schaal

Text © Linda Rae Schaal, Illustrations © Don Sidle

 Published by

RaeLin Press

For special ordering, please visit www.LindaRaeSchaal.com.
Burlington, CO, 80807

Book Design: Nick Zelinger, NZ Graphics
Book Consultant: Judith Briles, The Book Shepherd

ISBN: 978-1-955705-00-4 (print)
ISBN: 978-1-955705-02-8 (e-book)
ISBN: 978-1-955705-01-1 (audio)
Library of Congress Control Number: 2021912136

First Edition

Printed in the United States of America

For
Natalie Annaline Paul and Erna Christina Weisshaar
My Mother and Mother-in-Law
Two of the bravest women I know

"For wherever you go, I will go; and wherever you lodge, I will lodge.
Your people shall be my people, and your God, my God."
— Ruth 1:16 (NKJV)

I came upon a CATERPILLAR?

FISH

scurrying along

and I was about to stomp on her

Please don't end my life right here on this dusty old road.

I have been chased by a **BIRD**, a **CAT** and a **GRUMPY TOAD!**

Ribbit!

But you're so big and

POWERFUL,

I fear there is no way

that I can
outfox you.

Have mercy, sir, I

PRAY.

I turned around to make sure

that no one else could

that I was talking to
a bug,

and she was singing to me!

Then I figured, after all,

I could just let
her go.

She wasn't really hurting me.

No one would have to know.

When all at once our
eyes met

as we both turned
our heads.

Then both of us were giggling

till our faces were bright red!

At last we had to say goodbye
but as we walked away,
e knew that we would meet again
on another day.

Now I have a whole new point of view whenever I see critters.

I will simply let them go,

ABOUT THE AUTHOR AND THE ILLUSTRATOR

Linda Rae Schaal draws her inspiration for children's stories, poetry, musings and narratives from observations and real life experiences.

CLEA THE CLEVER CATERPILLAR and its sequels, CLEA'S RESCUE SQUAD, CLEA AND THE STORM and CLEA'S BIG SURPRISE blossomed through the 20 years she spent doting over her eight delightful and rambunctious grandchildren.

Linda's love of travel has taken her to thirty-two states and two continents. Her love of singing has taken her and her family all over the midwest, participating in fairs, festivals, churches, schools, nursing homes and jam sessions.

Discover more about Linda, her other books and the upcoming CLEA adventures on her website: www.LindaRaeSchaal.com.

Don Sidle is an illustrator/artist who lives with his wife Jamie and their rescue dog Quinn in Horseshoe Bay, Texas. After a career as an illustrator and editorial cartoonist he has changed his focus to capturing the unique landscape of the Texas hill country, and hopefully catch a few fish along the way.

MORE CLEA COMING SOON!

Who would think that the critters who scurry over the fields around us could be the very ones who would try to rescue a young monkey before it is too late? Clea calls on the strongest ones she knows, the soldier ants, but can they reach RJ and get back in time?

CLEA'S RESCUE SQUAD!

CLEA and the STORM!

A storm hits the fields and Clea and her friends scramble onto a log and are washed far away before the rains stop. Now they can't tell how to get home until a large turtle waddles by and Clea asks if he can help. But will he know the way and can they all hold on to his shell?

What could be such a big surprise when Clea has disappeared? RJ has brought his new friend, Chip, to meet the critters but no one knows where Clea is. Then they all see a new creature. Who could this be?

CLEA'S BIG SURPRISE!

THE JITTER SONG

Even if I happen to get the jitters;

even if I want to run away.

I won't be afraid of them;

we've become the best of friends.

I'm playing with the critters everyday;

Clea and the caterpillar way...

CPSIA information can be obtained
at www.ICGtesting.com
Printed in the USA
LVHW072058260722
724459LV00011B/341